The Dream Shop

by Katharine Kenah

Illustrated by Peter Catalanotto

H   HarperCollins Publishers

Special thanks to Nina and Josh—P.C.

The Dream Shop
Text copyright © 2002 by Katharine Kenah
Illustrations copyright © 2002 by Peter Catalanotto
Printed in Singapore. All rights reserved.
www.harperchildrens.com

Typography by Robbin Gourley
1 2 3 4 5 6 7 8 9 10
❖
First Edition

For Chris, with love,
and for J.W., a voice still heard

—K.K.

For Victor

—P.C.

Pip sat on her cot, listening to summer. The sleeping porch was too warm for sleep. The crickets were too loud. Too many fireflies glittered above the wheat. She took a drink of water and watched heat lightning marble the sky. Pip was hot and restless . . . until she remembered her cousin's words.

"There are places that are different from here," Joseph said. "Once upon a while, on an island above the ice and below the stars, there is a small shop made of wood where one can purchase dreams."

"Oh, I don't believe you," Pip said. But just in case, she asked, "How do you get there?"

Joseph glanced around the school bus, then whispered, "Squeeze your eyes shut tight and think about wooden horses prancing backwards."

On the sleeping porch, Pip squeezed her eyes shut tight and thought about wooden horses prancing backwards. Joseph never warned her about what happened next.

Suddenly Pip was in a small wooden shack that seemed to
grow from the inside. No matter what direction she walked,
through rows of tall shelves, she never could reach the farthest
wall. Outside the windows the ice wind was wild. But inside the
shack it was warm.

The aisles were full of dream shoppers in pajamas, staring and sorting through things on the shelves. "Help yourself," said a clerk in an apron. "Choose what you'd like to see in your dreams."

Pip found a baby pig the color of cream. She lifted it gently into her cart. There were music-box rabbits, jars of gemstones, and coloring books that drew themselves. When she reached for a sunset, boxed up and ready to blaze in her dreams, Pip saw Joseph coming down the aisle.

"What are you doing here?" he asked, surprised.

"Same as you, I guess," said Pip. "Shopping for my dreams."

Joseph looked in her cart. "Well, why are you choosing baby pigs and sunsets? We have those at home." He pointed to his cart. "I'm choosing *scarier* things," Joseph said. "I like exciting dreams."

Pip stared at his cart. There was a magician's box with no escape, a lion inside a submarine, and a tiny tornado in a cage. "I was just looking at the baby pig," said Pip, putting it back on the shelf. "You're not the only one who likes exciting dreams."

Pip pushed her cart past Joseph. The shelves got higher and wider and darker toward the back of the Dream Shop, where the contents of good dreams and bad dreams were mixed up together.

Knots of snakes slithered on the shelves. There were racks of bad report cards and unexpected tests. Surprise balls of secrets, like scoops of night sky, were wrapped in midnight blue paper dotted with stars. As Pip reached for one, Joseph was watching. So she stretched a bit farther for a carved mud statue with a mouth that screamed.

Joseph found an ancient map for explorers and waved it in Pip's face. "Look," he said, pointing to a swirling sea. "It says, *'Here Be Dragons.'*"

"You won't really find them," said Pip. "You'll just be dreaming."

Their carts were side by side when they saw a barrel ahead. People in bathrobes were poking into it and laughing. When the others left, Joseph and Pip stepped up to look. At the bottom was a small green dragon, pacing and gulping with soft snuffly sounds.

Pip looked at Joseph.

Joseph looked at Pip.

"He's *mine*," she said.

"I saw him first," said Joseph.

They leaned down and grabbed at the very same time, but Pip got him. The dragon felt soft and heavy in her hands . . . and cool like a grape.

"I got him," Pip cried. But when she pulled him up, the dragon burped a wisp of fire in her face and jumped from her arms. Then he raced off on short, bumpy legs, claws clicking on the smooth tiles of the Dream Shop floor.

"Get him!" said Joseph.

The dragon was scrambling straight for the aisle of
nightmares, bouncing like a rubber ball. He hit the display of
natural disasters at full speed, and the whole thing crashed to
the floor.

Bottles of lightning shattered to bits. Pip heard a moan that
was not wind; then the ground beneath them started to shake.
Earthquakes rolled like waves down the aisles.

"Run!" Pip yelled, but it was too late.

Customers were sliding and falling in their slippers. Thunder crashed through the store. Hailstones pelted and hurricanes poured.

Suddenly Pip saw the dragon bouncing their way. "Joseph," she called. "Open your map and set it on the floor! Get ready to grab him when I say, 'Now!'"

Joseph unrolled the map. Pip tugged a box from her cart. She pulled on its flaps and pried and yanked. Out popped a sunset. It dazzled the dragon with glorious light and stopped him cold.

"*Now!*" Pip shouted.

Joseph grabbed the dragon and set him onto the ancient map, on the swirly spot labeled *Here Be Dragons*. The Dream Shop dragon turned around three times, sneezed a puff of smoke, and vanished into the map. The storms stopped instantly.

Pip looked at Joseph.

Joseph looked at Pip.

"Let's go home," she said. "Squeeze your eyes shut tight and think about wooden horses prancing forwards."

Suddenly Pip was back on her cot, listening to summer . . .

when Joseph rode his bike out of the ocean of wheat and down the pebbly drive to her house.

"Hey," he called. "Come see what I have."

She ran off the porch. At the bottom of the handlebar basket was a baby pig the color of cream. They reached down at the very same time, but Pip got him first.

"He's yours," said Joseph.

"I know." Pip smiled at her cousin.

The baby pig felt soft and heavy in her hands . . .
and warm as a biscuit.